JUNIPER HOLLOW

Mr. Mole Moves In

Lesley-Anne Green

tundra

Tundra Books, an imprint of Penguin Random House Canada Young Readers, a
division of Penguin Random House of Canada Limited

Library and Archives Canada Cataloguing in Publication

Title: Mr. Mole moves in / Lesley-Anne Green.
Other titles: Mister Mole moves in
Names: Green, Lesley-Anne, 1977– author.
Identifiers: Canadiana (print) 20200182269 | Canadiana (ebook) 20200182277 |
ISBN 9781101918029 (hardcover) | ISBN 9781101918043 (EPUB) |
ISBN 978-0-7352-7116-6 (special markets)
Subjects: LCGFT: Picture books.
Classification: LCC PS8613.R42823 M7 2021 | DDC jC813/.6—dc23

Published simultaneously in the United States of America by Tundra Books of
Northern New York, an imprint of Penguin Random House Canada Young Readers, a
division of Penguin Random House of Canada Limited

Library of Congress Control Number: 2020933265

Edited by Samantha Swenson
Designed by Kate Sinclair and Kelly Hill
The artwork in this book was rendered in needle-felted wool, balsa wood and fabric.
The text was set in Plantin MT Pro.

Printed and bound in China

www.penguinrandomhouse.ca

1 2 3 4 5   25 24 23 22 21

Penguin
Random House
TUNDRA BOOKS

For Gus and Jeff

Mr. Mole had just moved to Juniper Hollow. He was looking forward to meeting his neighbors and making new friends.

Now, Juniper Hollow doesn't get too many new residents, so when they do, boy oh boy, do these critters get excited! That's why Raccoon had been playing in the grassy field by Mr. Mole's house waiting for a chance to meet him.

When he saw Mr. Mole emerge from his house that afternoon, Raccoon stopped his game of ball and rushed over to introduce himself.

"Hi! I'm Raccoon. It sure is nice to meet you," said Raccoon, sticking out his paw.

"I'm Mr. Mole. I just moved here from Mole Town. And the pleasure is all mine," said Mr. Mole, taking hold of a tree branch and giving it a good shake.

Raccoon was a little confused. "I guess that's how they do things in Mole Town," he said to himself.

He was still thinking about that paw shake when he ran into Rabbit and her bunnies on their way to town.

Raccoon told them all about meeting Mr. Mole. As they were chatting, they saw Mr. Mole heading their way, but instead of walking toward them, he walked right into a fence post.

"Oh, I beg your pardon," said Mr. Mole to the fence post.

"Did you hear how polite Mr. Mole was?" Rabbit said, turning to her bunnies.

"Yes, Mama!" they chorused.

"Mole Town must be a very polite place," said Rabbit approvingly.

She quickly hopped after Mr. Mole, hoping to introduce herself and her bunnies.

They had almost caught up to Mr. Mole when they saw him speaking with Giraffe outside the General Store. Of course, being a polite critter herself, Rabbit wasn't about to interrupt.

"What a beautiful baby!" Mr. Mole said, looking sweetly at the watermelon Giraffe was holding.

"Uh, thank you…?" said Giraffe, looking down at her watermelon. "Welcome to Juniper Hollow!" she added, but Mr. Mole had already gone inside the store.

Giraffe was feeling a little bewildered when Rabbit approached and told her everything that she had seen and heard about Mr. Mole that day.

"Well," said Giraffe, "they must really like watermelons in Mole Town."

"I guess so," agreed Rabbit.

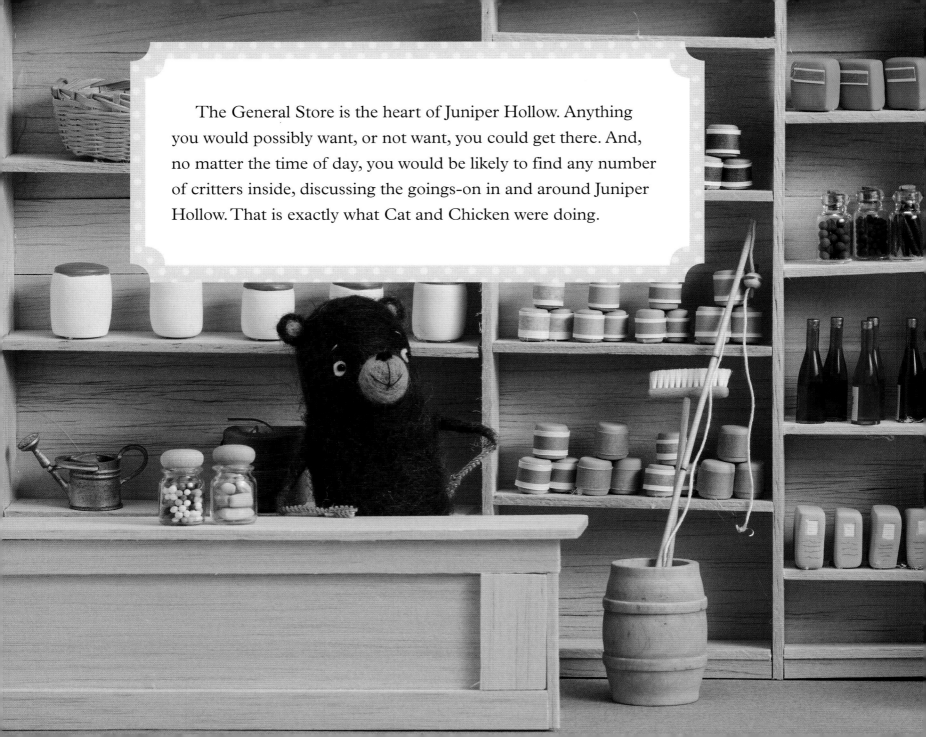

The General Store is the heart of Juniper Hollow. Anything you would possibly want, or not want, you could get there. And, no matter the time of day, you would be likely to find any number of critters inside, discussing the goings-on in and around Juniper Hollow. That is exactly what Cat and Chicken were doing.

"I saw that new critter, Mr. Mole, out walking today. He was wearing such a wonderful outfit!" said Cat enthusiastically.

"Mole Town must be very fashionable," said Chicken. "I hear that's where he moved from."

Cat was thinking about Mr. Mole's colorful sense of style when in walked Mr. Mole himself, followed by Rabbit and her bunnies.

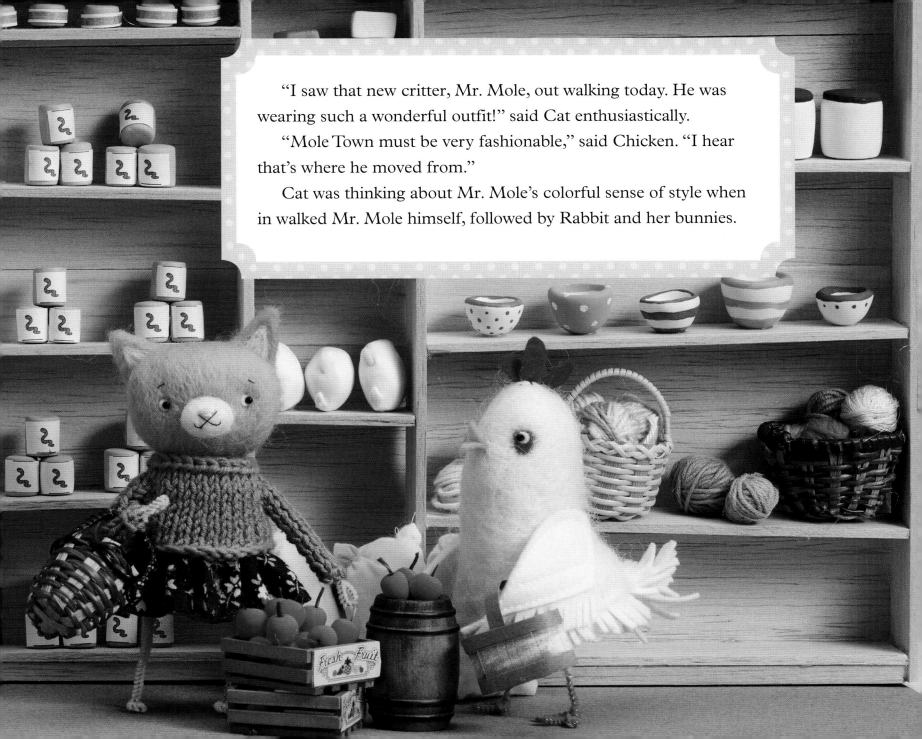

Inside, Mr. Mole began to fill his cart with cans of worms.

"Mmmm, delicious," he murmured.

"Can I interest you in a fishing rod to go with those?" asked Bear.

"No, thank you," said Mr. Mole. "I'm not much of a fisherman."

Bear wasn't sure what to make of that, but before he had a chance to ask questions, Rabbit hopped forward to introduce herself and her bunnies.

"Well, well, well!" exclaimed Mr. Mole. "How nice to meet you! Bear, I will also take three of these candies for the little ones," said Mr. Mole, dipping his paw into a jar on the counter. And with a smile, he handed each bunny an eraser and left the store with his groceries.

Rabbit considered the erasers for a moment.

"Maybe they chew them like bubble gum in Mole Town?" she said.

The bunnies weren't so sure about that. They decided they would save their "candies" for later — so as not to seem rude — and put them in their pockets.

"Mr. Mole seems like such a lovely critter," said Chicken, who had been watching from over by the canned goods.

"Oh yes!" agreed Cat. "We really should do something to welcome him to Juniper Hollow."

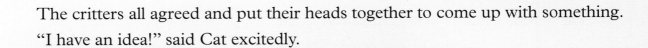

The critters all agreed and put their heads together to come up with something.
"I have an idea!" said Cat excitedly.
Word of Cat's plan spread like wildfire.

The next day, the critters of Juniper Hollow gathered together and made their way to Mr. Mole's house.

As they approached, they could see Mr. Mole peeking out from behind the curtains. They were surprised to find that he looked a little scared.

"Mr. Mole, it's just us critters come to welcome you to Juniper Hollow!" called Cat.

Mr. Mole opened his front door and stepped outside.

"We've brought you a welcome basket!" said Giraffe.

"Oh, how lovely!" said Mr. Mole, relieved they were a friendly mob.

"I also brought you these," said a tiny voice from the crowd. The littlest bunny hopped over to Mr. Mole and handed him her extra pair of glasses. "I thought maybe you could use them, " she said quietly.

"Oh my goodness!" exclaimed Mr. Mole. "How did you guess? I lost my glasses in the move, and I haven't been able to see a THING without them!"

Mr. Mole thanked everyone for the warm welcome, and as the crowd of critters dispersed, he took his welcome basket into the house.

Once inside, he eagerly opened the basket and found it filled with the most curious things. Branches? Erasers? A watermelon?!

Then he smiled to himself. "I guess that's just how they do things in Juniper Hollow."